R0200389344

07/2019

 W9-BJR-221

Dear Parents:

Congratulations! Your child is taking the first steps on an exciting journey. The destination? Independent reading!

STEP INTO READING® will help your child get there. The program offers five steps to reading success. Each step includes fun stories and colorful art or photographs. In addition to original fiction and books with favorite characters, there are Step into Reading Non-Fiction Readers, Phonics Readers and Boxed Sets, Sticker Readers, and Comic Readers—a complete literacy program with something to interest every child.

Learning to Read, Step by Step!

Ready to Read   Preschool–Kindergarten
• big type and easy words • rhyme and rhythm • picture clues
For children who know the alphabet and are eager to begin reading.

Reading with Help   Preschool–Grade 1
• basic vocabulary • short sentences • simple stories
For children who recognize familiar words and sound out new words with help.

Reading on Your Own   Grades 1–3
• engaging characters • easy-to-follow plots • popular topics
For children who are ready to read on their own.

Reading Paragraphs   Grades 2–3
• challenging vocabulary • short paragraphs • exciting stories
For newly independent readers who read simple sentences with confidence.

Ready for Chapters   Grades 2–4
• chapters • longer paragraphs • full-color art
For children who want to take the plunge into chapter books but still like colorful pictures.

STEP INTO READING® is designed to give every child a successful reading experience. The grade levels are only guides; children will progress through the steps at their own speed, developing confidence in their reading.

Remember, a lifetime love of reading starts with a single step!

Sisters Save the Day!

adapted by Kristen L. Depken
based on the original screenplay
by Grant Moran

Random House 🏠 New York

One day,

Barbie's dad has an idea.

Family time travel!

They will pretend to go
back in time.
They will pretend
to be pioneers!

That means no cars,
phones,
or electronics.
Skipper does *not*
like that.

Everyone else
is excited.

They try to change

Skipper's mind.

Skipper says yes.

Barbie and her family
set up a campsite
in the backyard.

They have tents
for sleeping.
They have a fire pit
for cooking.

Ken comes
to take pictures.
He brings a phone
for emergencies.

The girls turn
off their phones.
"Nooo!"
cries Skipper.

The family gets used
to pioneer life.
Barbie and Skipper
wash dishes by hand.

Chelsea and Stacie
play a clapping game.

At night,
the girls get bored.

Barbie teaches
them a song.
They have fun!

Oh no!
It starts
to rain.

The girls go
inside their tent.
The tent is leaking!
They are not happy.

The next morning,
Barbie and Skipper
walk to a farm
to get milk.
The milk is heavy.

The girls ride home
on the farm horse,
Misty.

They are very tired
when they get back!

Stacie and Chelsea
are tired, too.

Just then,
Barbie's mom gets
an emergency call.

Her work needs

a special project

right away.

There is too much traffic

to get it to the office

in time.

Barbie has an idea.

She and Skipper

will ride Misty

to their mom's work.

Pioneers did not
have traffic.
They will not
have traffic either!

The girls take
the project and ride
to the office.
They ride
up the escalator.

They ride

in the elevator.

They get the project
to the boss in time!

"Thank you!"
says their mom
when they get home.

Barbie, Skipper,
and Misty
saved the day!

Pioneer life
is not so bad
after all!